W9-BRB-785

Purchased from
Multnomah County Library
Title Wave Used Bookstore
216 NE Knott St, Portland, OR
503-988-5021

Brother Juniper

BY
Diane Gibfried

ILLUSTRATED BY
Meilo So

CLARION BOOKS / NEW YORK

To Mom and Dad, and Junipers everywhere

—D.G.

To Uncle Mike

—M.S.

$\mathcal{B}$rother Juniper was a holy friar.
He lived in the hills of Assisi with Father Francis
and seven other brothers.

There was

Brother
Giles

Brother
Elias

Brother
Pietro

Brother
Silvester

Brother
Leo

Brother
Bernard

and Brother
Masseo.

6

They worked together. They prayed together. Sometimes they begged
for food. Sometimes they had none.

Brother Juniper was the most generous of the brothers. Father Francis loved him because he was simple.

The other brothers knew he was good. But some of them thought he was silly.

This was because Brother Juniper was
often naked.

If somebody asked him for his robe,
Brother Juniper would gladly give it
to him.

Even if it was a cold day. Even if
it was snowing.

One day, Father Francis said, "Brother Juniper, we are going out to preach. Will you stay home and watch the chapel?"

"Yes," said Brother Juniper.

The other brothers were worried about leaving Brother Juniper at the chapel. They knew how generous he could be.

But they did as Father Francis told them and
headed down the mountain.
Brother Juniper waved goodbye.

He prayed for a while.

And then he cleaned.

He polished the
golden candlesticks.

He dusted the
golden chalice.

He washed the embroidered altar cloth.

He mended the
brocade vestments.

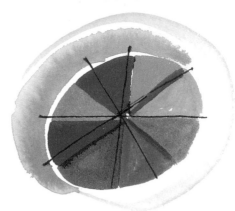

He scrubbed the door and
the stained glass windows until
the whole chapel was shiny
and bright.

He sat down for a moment to rest, when . . .
Knock, knock, knock!

Brother Juniper opened the door.
A poor old man stood outside.
"Hello," said Brother Juniper.
"Can you help me?" said the old man.
"I am so old that I am losing my sight. I
cannot see well enough to work at my job
repairing shoes. Soon I will go hungry."

Brother Juniper picked up the golden candlesticks.

"Take these," he said. "If you sell them, you can buy some spectacles."

"Thank you," said the old man, and he went on his way.

Brother Juniper was glad he could help. He was singing about it, when . . .

Knock, knock, knock!

Brother Juniper opened the door.

A woman and her eight children stood outside.

"My husband is sick, and I cannot feed my children on my own poor wages."

Brother Juniper handed her the golden chalice.

"If you sell this, you can eat for a while," he said. "Your husband can rest and get better."

"Thank you," the woman said, and she went on her way. Brother Juniper was glad that he had cleaned everything that morning.

Word must have spread fast.
All day long Brother Juniper
was busy giving things away.

He gave the altar cloth to
a baker to cover his basket of
warm bread.

He gave the vestments to
a raggedy young artist.

He even gave the door to a
family whose house had been
wrecked in a storm.

By evening, there were no walls,
no windows, and no door.
Nothing except Brother Juniper
and his broom.
Until . . .

. . . a cleaning woman came and said, "I have
no broom and I cannot sweep."

So Brother Juniper gave her his broom.

And she was shivering. So he gave her
his robe.

When the other brothers came home, they found Brother Juniper standing naked in an empty hole.

"Where is the church?" shouted Brother Masseo.

"You have torn it down!" cried Brother Silvester.

"You have ruined our church!" shouted Brother Bernard.

"Where will we worship?" asked Brother Pietro.

Brother Juniper was sad.

He hid himself and didn't come out until Sunday, because on Sunday it was his job to ring the bell.

But he had given the bell to a teacher who wanted to start a school.

So instead, Brother Juniper stood on a rock and shouted,

DING, DING, DING

All the brothers came with long faces.
They were standing in the hole together when . . .

. . . over the hill came an old man with new spectacles.

And after him came a woman with eight smiling children.

After her came a baker with a basket of warm, fresh bread,
and a raggedy artist dressed in nice new clothes,

26

and a teacher with a group of school children . . .
and their parents . . .
and their grandparents.

A huge crowd gathered around Brother Juniper.
Everyone smiled, and one child said, "We just
came to say thank you!"

The other brothers looked at the
crowd and were amazed.

When Father Francis arrived, he smiled a great big smile at Brother Juniper.

"Look, Brothers, at the fine church that Brother Juniper built. I wish I had a forest of these Junipers."

AUTHOR'S NOTE

This story was inspired by traditional tales about Brother Juniper, a friar and a friend of St. Francis of Assisi. Though little is known about Brother Juniper, we do know that he joined St. Francis and his followers in 1210 and that he died in 1258. Through the years, stories about St. Francis and his companions were told in order to teach about his spiritual way of life. These stories were collected in The Little Flowers of St. Francis, *and I have adapted themes from that book for the purposes of creating my own original story here.*

Clarion Books
a Houghton Mifflin Company imprint
215 Park Avenue South, New York, NY 10003

Text copyright © 2006 by Diane Gibfried
Illustrations copyright © 2006 by Meilo So

The illustrations were executed in watercolor, colored ink and gouache.
The text was set in 13.5-point Miller Text.

All rights reserved.

For information about permission to reproduce selections from this book, write to
Permissions, Houghton Mifflin Company, 215 Park Avenue South, New York, NY 10003.

www.houghtonmifflinbooks.com

Manufactured in China

Library of Congress Cataloging-in-Publication Data

Gibfried, Diane.
Brother Juniper / by Diane Gibfried ; illustrated by Meilo So.
p. cm.
Summary: Worried about having left the overly generous Brother Juniper in charge
of their chapel when they went out to preach, the other friars are not prepared for
what they find upon their return.
ISBN-10: 0-618-54361-9
ISBN-13: 978-0-618-54361-8
[1. Generosity—Fiction. 2. Friars—Fiction. 3. Francis, of Assisi, Saint, 1182–1226—Fiction.]
I. So, Meilo, ill. II. Title.
PZ7.G3392533Br 2006   [E]—dc22   2005010038

SCP 10 9 8 7 6 5 4 3 2 1